The Dollhouse Magic

THE DOLLHOUSE MAGIC

Yona Zeldis McDonough

with illustrations by

Diane Palmisciano

AN
APPLE
PAPERBACK

SCHOLASTIC INC.
New York Toronto London Auckland Sydney
Mexico City New Delhi Hong Kong Buenos Aires

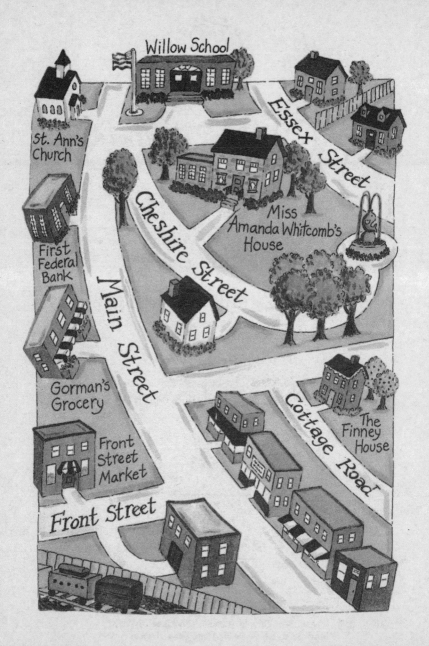

The Dollhouse Magic

ISBN 0-439-34049-7

Text copyright © 2000 by Yona Zeldis McDonough.
Illustrations copyright © 2000 by Diane Palmisciano.
All rights reserved. Published by Scholastic Inc., 555 Broadway, New York, NY
10012 by arrangement with Henry Holt and Company, LLC. SCHOLASTIC and
associated logos are trademarks and/or registered trademarks of Scholastic Inc.

12 11 10 9 8 7 6 5 4 3 2 1   1 2 3 4 5 6/0

Printed in the U.S.A.   40

First Scholastic printing, November 2001

Contents

The Dollhouse Magic

Little House, Big House

Of all the streets in town, Lila and Jane Finney like Cheshire the very best. It's not because of the large old oaks whose spreading branches arch and nearly meet in the air, creating, in spring and summer, a most beguiling canopy overhead. Nor is it the well-tended flower beds, though these are filled with an ongoing seasonal display: tulips and daffodils in spring; roses, lilies, and marigolds in summer; asters and mums in the fall. It is not even because of the way the street ends in a lush, grassy circle, in the center of which is a handsomely carved old stone fountain. No, as attractive as all these things are, what Lila and Jane love most is a house on Cheshire Street, a three-story dollhouse with real clapboard siding and a cedar shingle roof that sits in Miss Amanda Whitcomb's front window.

The dollhouse, which is painted a deep crimson color, has a large central structure flanked by two identical smaller wings. There is a pillared porch and second-story veranda that extends all along the front, with little carved posts and a tiny wooden railing around it. "So the dolls won't fall down and get hurt," explains Lila gravely. "That would be terrible."

Lila is the serious one, the one who always thinks of these things. Jane knows this by now, so she just nods in assent. Real shutters frame all seventeen of the mullioned

windows, which are hung with ivory lace curtains. The porch and shutters are painted dove gray, and the front door is Wedgwood blue.

When they get to the corner of Cheshire Street, Lila and Jane begin a slow trot down the block. The best time of day is right at dusk, for sometimes—but not always—Miss Whitcomb lights the tiny candles that stand in their brass candleholders. The flames, though ever so small, seem to light up the darkness in such a cheerful way.

"What do you think Mr. Montgomery will be doing today?" says Jane, who is two years younger than Lila and has to hurry to keep up. "Last time he was in the downstairs parlor, playing checkers with Mrs. Montgomery."

Mr. and Mrs. Montgomery are the names Lila and Jane have given two of the dolls that live in Miss Whitcomb's dollhouse. They are very well made and precious, with finely modeled bisque faces, glass eyes, and real mohair wigs, not just hair that was painted on their heads. Lila always says the dolls look old, and Jane agrees. But they do look well tended to. In the past, Lila has pointed out how bits of their faces were carefully repainted and how parts of their clothing had been mended; if you looked very hard, you could see that the thread was sometimes a slightly different color.

In addition to Mr. and Mrs. Montgomery—he with a black felt jacket, black-and-white houndstooth check trousers, and olive green silk vest; she with a long scarlet dress that had tiny bugle beads decorating the front and a real lace collar—there were several other dolls. The girls named a pretty young woman doll Cousin Cassandra. She had pale yellow hair and a dress of cornflower blue and white gingham. Jane liked her the best. There was also a doll who had the dark uniform and white apron of a cook, whom they named Trudy, and another with a pale blue uniform whom they simply called Nanny. Both Lila and Jane felt she belonged in the second-floor nursery, the one whose wallpaper showed pink and blue bunnies and that had a miniature wooden rocking horse set atop the braided rug. Two more dolls were the grandmother and grandfather; they had gray hair and both wore black spectacles. There were even pets: a calico cat and spotted dog, both made of porcelain. But of all the dolls who lived in the house, none were children.

"Don't you think it's odd that there are no children?" remarks Lila to her sister, and Jane has to agree that she does. But right now, Lila is thinking about something else. "It might be the front that we see today," she reminds Jane. "We've seen the inside the last three times, remember?"

Because Miss Whitcomb's parlor window was so big and the dollhouse so close to it, the girls had noticed that the dollhouse sat on a revolving disk. Sometimes Miss Whitcomb faced the inside of the house out toward the street; other times, she faced the facade outward. Either way, the girls love to see how she rearranges and changes it to fit in perfectly with the seasons.

Last summer, she had put tiny terra-cotta pots of silk geraniums by the front door and real wicker furniture—a settee, two chairs, and a table—on the porch. The table held a small glass pitcher and four small tumblers on a pewter tray. "There should be lemonade in the pitcher," Jane had said. "If it were ours, we could fill it up when Mama makes lemonade in the summer."

"And ice too," Lila offered. "We could grind up a chunk from the icebox and make tiny little slivers to go inside. It would look so real!"

"It would be wonderful," said Jane. "Truly wonderful."

This past fall, the wicker furniture and terra-cotta pots were put away and replaced with a pair of pumpkins that sat on either side of the front door. "What do you think they're made of?" Jane had asked.

"Maybe wax? Or papier-mâché?" answered Lila, who knew about such things. Jane often asked her questions, confident that somehow Lila would know the answers. But even Lila wasn't sure about the pumpkins. The girls had never been any nearer to the dollhouse than the outside of Miss Whitcomb's window. They had never seen any of the tiny treasures up close or held them in their hands.

By the time Lila and Jane reach the house today, they are a little out of breath. Although it is late November, the air is surprisingly mild and they feel overheated in their scarves, winter coats, and mittens.

"Oh, look! It's the outside today!" says Lila. "There's a wreath on the door!"

"I can see the Christmas tree inside," Jane adds. "But it's not decorated yet. And there aren't any presents."

"That comes later," says Lila. "In December." She presses her face against the window, straining to see the tree through the front windows of the dollhouse. Maybe there are presents after all. Jane comes up right beside her, pulling on a lock of her light brown hair. Her hair is, as always, rather untidy, with lots of wisps standing out around her face. The girls are so entranced that they don't hear the door open.

"Well, hello," says the old woman in the doorway. "Who might you be?"

For a moment, the girls cannot answer but just stand

silently. The woman's voice and words are certainly kind enough, but her appearance is more than a little odd. Her long white hair is worn in two tightly bound braids that hang down her back—much longer than Lila's neat blond ones, which Jane has always envied. Then there are her unusual clothes: a long, heavily patterned skirt; a paisley wool shawl of red, black, and gold; and a pair of dangling earrings with amber beads that sparkle in the light. The woman's face, though clearly old, has a lively, engaging look, and her light blue eyes seem to be gazing carefully at the girls. Lila realizes with embarrassment that they are staring. She quickly recovers and introduces them both.

"Well, Lila and Jane Finney," says the old woman, "I'm Amanda Whitcomb. I have to confess I've seen you here before."

"That's true," mumbles Lila, wishing they had taken more care not to be seen.

Jane is holding her hand tightly, a little afraid that they are in trouble.

"Oh, but that's fine!" assures Miss Whitcomb. "You just wanted to see the dollhouse. Isn't that right?"

"Yes, ma'am, that's it," says Lila.

"Then maybe you'd like to come in and have a closer look," suggests Miss Whitcomb with a smile.

Lila and Jane look at each other. Go inside! See the dollhouse right up close. How extraordinary! But what had their mother told them about strangers? Even though Miss Whitcomb seemed very nice, they didn't really know her.

"We would love to come in, Miss Whitcomb," answers Lila, trying not to sound too disappointed. "But we should ask our mother first."

"That's a good idea," Miss Whitcomb replies. "I can see you're a sensible girl." Lila relaxes a little and actually smiles.

"If your mother says it's all right," continues Miss Whitcomb, "you can come by tomorrow, around half-past three. I'll have some cider and cookies waiting too."

"We'll go ask her right now!" pipes up Jane, tugging at Lila's sleeve to get going.

"Thank you very much," Lila says, letting herself be led

away by her sister. Then she turned and followed Jane, who had by now let go of her hand and was already well ahead. Lila knew she was heading for their favorite shortcut—a narrow footpath that cut through the oak trees by the fountain—and she raced along to catch up.

Old House, New House

Home for Lila and Jane was in the southern part of town, closer to the railroad tracks. This had not always been so. Before the hard times came, the Finneys had lived in a yellow house on Essex Street, not too far from where Miss Whitcomb lived. Daddy had worked at the First Federal Savings and Loan bank downtown. Every day he wore a three-piece suit with a silk bow tie. In his vest pocket he carried a beautiful silver pocket watch that had belonged to his grandfather; sometimes he let Lila, Jane, or one of the boys hold the watch very close to their ears so they could hear its musical ticking.

In the house on Essex Street, Lila and Jane had a room of their own, with matching twin beds and dressers. Their two older brothers, Henry and William, shared another room, and baby Annabelle slept with Mama and Daddy. There was a kitchen with a pantry and a parlor and a dining room downstairs. They had lilac bushes and a rabbit hutch in the backyard; there was even a covered front porch with a wooden swing. Lila and Jane loved to sit in the swing on summer nights, telling each other long, involved stories about princesses and castles. Sometimes they fell asleep there, and Daddy had to carry them up to bed.

But when the Depression came, all that changed. Daddy lost his job at the bank, and soon they lost their house too. The silver pocket watch, their bedroom furniture, Mama's wedding china, and lots of other things were sold to help pay the bills. The Finneys moved into the cramped bottom floor of a run-down house on Cottage Road. Mama said, "It's only for a while, until Daddy gets back on his feet and finds another job."

Mama did her best to clean the old place up. With the children's help, she cleared the cobwebs from the corners and swept the mouse droppings that littered the floor. The dirty kitchen was scrubbed with her special pine-scented soap. Gingham dish towels were tacked up as curtains. Some old furniture had been left in the house, so Mama covered the torn sofa with a tablecloth and sewed more curtains from their bedsheets.

At first, all the children missed the other house so much that they couldn't find anything to like about the new one. But gradually, they began to notice things about it like the ornate gingerbread trim that ran all the way around the roof. Papa decided to paint the trim with a fresh coat of white, and all the children helped. Painting was lots of fun, kind of like dipping your brush into a big can of cream. After it was done, Mama gave them morning glory seeds to plant outside, and when the blue flowers wound their way up and around the newly painted white wood, the girls had to admit it looked fine indeed.

Then there were the two cherry trees in the backyard; come summer, their branches grew heavy with dark red fruit. Lila and Jane formed one team and Henry and William formed another; they tried to beat each other in picking the most cherries. Mama declared them all winners and baked six cherry pies for prizes. In fact, there were so many cherries that she made preserves too. Rich and sweet, a spoonful turned an ordinary piece of bread into dessert. "This is so good, you could sell it!" Daddy exclaimed the first time he had a taste. The children all laughed, but don't you know that Mama went and did just that! Batches and batches of cherry preserves, all neatly bottled and labeled were sold to her friends and neighbors every week.

Now, as Jane and Lila came running into the yard, they see Daddy gathering sticks for the wood-burning stove in the kitchen. The stove is something else the girls found to like. On cold afternoons the smell of the chimney smoke makes them feel warm before they even get inside.

"Daddy! Daddy!" cries Jane. "Where's Mama? We have to find her!"

"Whoa!" Daddy laughs. Like everyone else in the Finney family, he knows how excitable Jane is. "How about a hello first?"

"We're sorry," says Lila, who reaches up to hug him.

"Mama's inside, fixing supper," Daddy tells her. "Maybe you want to go in and help." Lila and Jane find Mama standing with her back to them at the stove, where she is stirring a large pot of soup.

"Hello, girls." Mama turns around and smiles.

"Mama, do you know Miss Whitcomb?" asks Jane in a big rush. "Her house is on Cheshire Street."

"Everybody in town knows Miss Whitcomb," says Mama. "She taught music at the high school for years. And gave private lessons when she retired."

"So you know her? She's not a stranger?"

"I don't know her well, but no, I wouldn't say she's a stranger."

"Wouldn't say who's a stranger?" Daddy asks, coming into the room. His arms are filled with twigs.

"Miss Whitcomb. Over on Cheshire Street," explains Mama.

"Amanda Whitcomb? I know her from the bank. She took her money out just before the bank failed; almost like she had a sixth sense about it. I always did like her. She used to bring a fruitcake over to the bank at Christmastime. She made it herself, with brandy and lots of dates."

"Then we can go see her tomorrow? After school?" begs Jane, who is not at all interested in the bank or the fruitcake.

"What's all this about?" says Mama, looking from one girl to the other. So they tell her about the invitation and watch as she and Daddy exchange those grown-up looks.

"Well, I don't see why not," Mama says, and Daddy nods in agreement. "But you'll have to mind your manners. Jane, that means no playing with your food. And Lila, you remember to say please and thank you. Promise?"

"Promise!" chorus Jane and Lila in unison.

That night, Jane and Lila have trouble falling asleep. Now that they share a room with William and Henry (two sets of twin beds, nearly side by side), things are pretty lively at bedtime. Sometimes William tells scary stories about witches, goblins, and ghosts. The stories are very complicated and often echo the serial radio programs the children listen to in the evening. Then there is Henry's snoring, and William is always getting up: for a glass of water, to go to the bathroom, to open the window or to close it.

But tonight it's not the spooky stories or interruptions that keep them awake. No, instead they are excited about tomorrow's adventure, and when Lila is sure the boys are sleeping, she invites Jane over to her bed so that they can whisper without Mama and Daddy hearing.

"Do you think she'll let us see it?" asks Jane for what must be the tenth time that night.

"Of course, silly. That's why she invited us, remember?"

"How about touching? Will she let us touch anything?

I really want to hold Cassandra in my hands."

"Maybe," says Lila. "But we'll have to be good.
Mama said so."

"Oh, I will!" says Jane.

"Are you sure you can
behave?"

"Yes, I'm sure,"
says Jane, starting
to feel annoyed. "But
you don't have to boss
me around, you know."

"I'm not bossing. Just telling. And would you move over—you're hogging the blanket!" Lila says.

"Am not!"

"Are too!"

There is a short, tense silence.

"Here's your old blanket," says Jane finally. "Can I stay here with you if I promise not to take it?"

"All right," says Lila. "But let's go to sleep. I'm tired."

"Me too." Jane yawns. "And I want to dream about the dollhouse."

Cider, Cookies, and Candy

The next day is much colder, and the girls shiver on their way to school. Lila heads upstairs to the fourth-grade classroom, while Jane goes down a long hall to the second-grade classroom. Jane is not looking forward to school today and not only because she can't wait until half-past three. There is also the matter of the dress she is wearing. It's one of Lila's old dresses, made of navy blue wool, with a Peter Pan collar and pleats all around. The elbows were mended not once but twice, and its hem had been let down at least that many times. Even though there are several other girls in her class who also wear hand-me-down clothes, for some reason she is the only one who is teased. Maybe that's because dresses—whether new or secondhand—quickly assume a sloppy, well-worn look when Jane puts them on. She's always finding mysterious stains or little rips. And no matter how hard she tries, everything she wears seems to wrinkle instantly. Tall, slender Lila always manages to look neat, whereas she . . . Jane sighs just thinking about it.

But today things go better than Jane expects. She wins the class spelling bee and receives a red ribbon that says Number One in gold letters in the center. Her teacher helps her pin it to her dress, and next to the shiny red satin the blue wool dress doesn't look so bad after all. Then Jane finds three pennies in the school yard at recess, which she shows no one but stuffs down into the bottom of her pocket to share with Lila after school.

Later, while her class is doing arithmetic and geography, Jane reaches into her pocket, where the pennies glow in secret. Before they go to Cheshire Street, she and Lila can make a stop at Gorman's Grocery for some candy. Sour balls are two for a penny; red-and-white peppermints are three. There are also red-hot dollars, licorice twists, peanut chews, chocolate bears, lollipops, and gumdrops. Jane can hardly wait.

Finally school is over, and she and Lila are making their way to Miss Whitcomb's. When Jane pulls out the pennies, Lila is dumbfounded. "Where did they come from?" she asks. "You didn't steal them, did you?"

"Of course not!" Jane tells Lila the story, and Lila marvels over her luck.

Gorman's Grocery is warm and cozy after the frigid air outside, and the girls take a long time deciding how to spend their windfall. Before they leave, they have purchased four chocolate bears—Jane loves how chewy they are and how long they last—two lollies, and four gumdrops, two red and two orange. They haven't had candy in a long while, so this is a big treat. But right before Jane is about to pop the first gumdrop into her mouth, Lila says, "Wait!"

"What is it?" Jane asks crossly.

"We need a present."

"A present?" repeats Jane.

"For Miss Whitcomb. You know, Mama always says that when you go to someone's house, it's nice to bring a present."

"She didn't say we had to," argues Jane, who can see where this is leading.

"No, but still. We should," says Lila.

"Well, we don't have one." Jane is defiant.

"Yes, we do," Lila points out. "You're holding it."

"Not our candy!" protests Jane.

"Maybe not all of it," concedes Lila. "But something. A gumdrop and a chocolate bear. From each of us."

"Do we have to?" Jane asks.

"We have to," Lila says firmly.

"Well, I won't." Jane stops walking and holds her candy tightly in her hand.

"Jane, Mama said you have to listen to me. Otherwise we can't go." The two sisters glare at each other for a moment until Jane says, "Lila, you look funny with your face all scrunched up like that," which makes them both laugh. Then Jane adds, "Oh, I guess one gumdrop won't be so bad."

"And a bear," Lila reminds her while Jane pops the gumdrop she has been holding into her mouth. It's the orange one, her favorite, and she tries to make it last a long, long time.

* * *

Miss Whitcomb answers the bell almost at once. On the way over, the girls talked about her unusual clothes and agreed that they would not stare, no matter what she is wearing. Still, they are not prepared for the thick skirt of red felt that she has on, nor the fuzzy red mohair cardigan, whose buttons are all different shapes: one is a flower, another a heart, a third is a rabbit, and the one right under her chin is a frog. Jane wishes she knew where Miss Whitcomb found such buttons; she would love to buy some and add them to Mama's button box. Then when she lost a plain blue or black one, it could be replaced by a star, a flower, or a frog!

"Come in, come in," says Miss Whitcomb, gathering their coats and things. "I can heat the cider a bit. Would you like that?"

"Oh yes, please!" says Lila. They look around the front hall for a moment. To one side is the dining room and beyond that the kitchen. To the other is the parlor.

"Why don't you go in and have a look?" says Miss Whitcomb, following the direction of Lila's gaze. "I'll just go and put a flame under that cider."

"Can we really?" asks Jane, her voice almost a squeal.

"Yes, you can," says Miss Whitcomb, and she leads them into the room. "Which way shall I turn it?" and before they can answer, she swings the house around so that the rooms are facing the girls. "You'll want to see the inside, of course." She pulls up small stools that are nearby. "I'll be back soon."

"I can't believe it," whispers Jane when they are alone.

"Neither can I," says Lila. The dollhouse is, close up, even more wonderful than they have imagined. On the ground floor is a narrow front hall, with real wooden parquet flooring. To the right is the big parlor, with a carved mantel and red flocked wallpaper. Beyond that is the little study, the one that has the game table where Mr. Montgomery likes to sit and play checkers. Though today he is sitting in the tapestry-covered armchair, reading a minuscule newspaper.

"Maybe his feet should be up. On the ottoman," suggests Jane quietly. "That's what Daddy likes to do when he reads the paper."

"That's a good idea," says Lila. "But we better ask before we touch anything."

To the left of the hallway is the dining room, where Cook

is setting the table for dinner. Hand-painted plates are on the table, and in the center is a glass bowl with silk flowers. The kitchen is right beyond that, and the evidence of cooking is strewn all about: there are several yellowware bowls, the kind Mama uses, on the counters, and a rolling pin has been left on the table. The big black stove has some copper pots on the burners, and there is a perfectly rendered little ham with a slice of pineapple on a silvery platter, just waiting to be brought into the dining room. Upstairs, in the small dressing room that adjoins the master bedroom, Mrs. Montgomery is seated at her dressing table. "Probably combing her hair before dinner," explains Lila.

"Look, she's been shopping!" says Jane, pointing to three tiny hatboxes piled atop one another on the floor. "Do you think they have hats inside?"

"Actually, they do. Would you like to take a look?" Jane and Lila turn abruptly to see Miss Whitcomb standing behind them, arms outstretched under a big wooden tray. It holds three steaming cups of cider and a round plate piled high with cookies.

"Could we?" asks Lila. "We didn't want to touch without asking."

"But of course you may touch. I think the whole fun is in the touching. Don't you?"

So Lila carefully lifts off the cover of the hatbox to reveal a tiny black felt hat inside, decorated with the narrowest band of black ribbon and three scarlet flowers. "To go with her dress!" exclaims Jane.

Miss Whitcomb puts the tray down on a table, and they eat their snack in the parlor. In between bites of the molasses cookies and sips of the spiced cider, the girls tell her about their family, the house on Essex Street where they used to live, and the one on Cottage Road where they live now. Miss Whitcomb nods and smiles as they talk. When they've finished eating, they all three turn their attention back to the dollhouse, for Miss Whitcomb pulls up another stool and joins them in their play.

"So many of these things were mine when I was a girl," she says, holding Cassandra in her hands. "This doll was always my favorite."

"Mine too!" says Jane. She fairly glows when Miss Whitcomb places it in her hands with the words, "Then you must get to play with her too." It is this gesture that gives Jane the courage to add, "But Lila and I always wonder why

there are no children dolls. No little girls or boys or babies. There's a nursery, after all. Who lives there?"

Miss Whitcomb is silent for a long moment, and Lila worries that Jane has offended her. But when she speaks, her voice is kind. "You're right, you know," she says. "There were some little children a long time ago. But I can't think of what's become of them. Maybe I'll have to find some others—a house needs children, after all."

The girls stay until the sky turns dark; they are pleasantly full from the cookies and so enchanted by the dollhouse that they forget the time entirely. It is only when Miss Whitcomb looks at her watch and says, "Oh, my! It's nearly five-thirty! We don't want your parents to worry," that Jane and Lila remember. Lila jumps up quickly; she knows Mama will be annoyed if they are late for supper.

"You'd better hurry," she says to Jane, who is still seated and gazing at the dollhouse. Reluctantly Jane stands up and, without thinking, utters a tiny burp. Lila elbows her quickly, reminding her of her manners.

"Excuse me," Jane murmurs, looking down at the floor.

"Maybe you girls would like some cookies to take home," says Miss Whitcomb, who seems not to have heard this. "To

share with your brothers. I have plenty more in the kitchen."
Suddenly Jane remembers what they have brought for her
and reaches into her pocket.

"Here," she says, a little awkwardly. "We forgot to give
you these before." She hands Miss Whitcomb the gumdrop
and the chocolate bear, both covered with a faint coating
of lint.

"That's right," adds Lila, proud that Jane was the one
who remembered. She plans to tell Mama about it when they
get home. But right now, she gives her two candies to Miss
Whitcomb, who holds all the pieces cupped in her hands.

"Why, thank you so much," Miss Whitcomb says, looking from one girl to the other. "Was there a party at school
today?"

"Oh no," says Jane, and she explains about finding the
pennies and stopping at Gorman's.

"I see," says Miss Whitcomb seriously. "Well, I will certainly enjoy them. Now, how about those cookies?" Lila and
Jane smile and nod eagerly. Miss Whitcomb disappears into
the kitchen as they get into their coats and hats. They button,
snap, and tie everything snugly, for the walk home will be
cold. Jane has trouble with the top button, so Lila buttons it

for her. When Miss Whitcomb returns, she hands them a large paper bag. Lila thanks her and takes the bag, which is heavier than she expected; her arms droop momentarily with the weight.

"I put a box of butterscotch toffees in there too," says Miss Whitcomb. "They were a gift from my niece Margaret. She lives in New York City. I wouldn't want to hurt her feelings, but I never did care much for butterscotch."

"We love butterscotch!" Jane beams, and together she and Lila follow Miss Whitcomb to the front door.

"Well, isn't that a lucky coincidence," says Miss Whitcomb as she leans upon the doorjamb. "Now, will you come again and tell me if your brothers liked the cookies?" she adds.

"We will!" says Jane as she and Lila head out into the frosty evening.

As it turns out, William and Henry like the cookies so much that Jane doesn't even get to eat one; the boys have polished them off before she has a chance. "No fair!" she cries, looking from the crumbs on Henry's face to the empty plate.

"Henry!" says Mama sharply. "You mean to say you ate them all?"

"Not by myself!" he protests. "William and Lila had some too."

Mama sighs. "Well, I'd like you all to apologize to your sister. Next time, I guess I have to be the one to divide the cookies."

"At least there's still the butterscotch," says Jane, but she says it softly, to herself.

Christmas Is Coming

After that magical afternoon, Lila and Jane become frequent visitors to the house on Cheshire Street. They get to know the dollhouse better than they ever would have imagined. They open every tiny drawer, inspect the contents of every miniature cupboard. Sometimes they even make their own suggestions or additions, like the time that Lila borrowed Daddy's knife and shaved down a bunch of twigs Jane had gathered to make logs for the fireplace. Or the afghan throw Mama helped Lila knit out of scraps of wool from her yarn basket. Miss Whitcomb is delighted by these additions to the house. "It hasn't been played with or enjoyed for such a long time," she says wistfully.

"But don't you rearrange things and play with it a bit?" asks Jane timidly.

"Yes, dear, I do," says Miss Whitcomb. "But I was thinking about children. Children are what give a dollhouse its life and its magic, you know."

"Who was the last child who played with it?" Lila asks.

"My niece Margaret. The one who lives in New York. But that was a long time ago. She's all grown up now."

One afternoon, shortly before the girls are ready to go, Miss Whitcomb shows them a box filled with dollhouse furniture and other things that have been broken through years of use and play. "I was hoping to find some little girl or boy dolls in the attic," she explains. "Instead I found this."

"I'll bet Daddy could fix these things," says Jane, holding a table with a missing leg in her hand. "He's very good at that."

"Is he really?" Miss Whitcomb says.

"Oh yes. When we lived in our other house, he had a wood shop out back, in the shed. He used to fix things all the time.

And make things too." One Christmas, Daddy had made two doll cradles, one for her and one for Lila. Another Christmas, he had made the boys a great big castle, with turrets and towers and a drawbridge that you could really lower and raise. Lila and Jane had loved it too.

"So he doesn't make or fix things anymore?" Miss Whitcomb was asking, interrupting Jane's reverie.

"Well, he doesn't have the shop now. And he says the wood is expensive."

"So it is," says Miss Whitcomb.

"He's awfully busy too," adds Lila.

"Oh?"

"He works down at the market on Front Street. Lifting boxes and things like that," Jane says proudly. Even though it's not the same as working in a bank, Jane is glad he has a job, especially when there are so many people out of work.

"I see," says Miss Whitcomb. She sips delicately from her cup of tea; the girls are drinking hot cocoa. "Say, I have an idea. Do you think your father would like to try fixing these things for me? I would pay him, of course." She looks eagerly from Lila to Jane.

"Well, I'm not sure," begins Lila.

"He would, I know he would!" interrupts Jane. "Oh, let's bring the box home, Lila! Let's ask him!"

"I guess we could," Lila says uncertainly, and so they do.

Walking back home in the wintry dusk, Jane asks Lila why she was so reluctant to bring Daddy the furniture. "It's just that he works all the time," she explains. "I didn't want to give him something else to do."

But when they show Daddy the box, Lila can see that he is interested by the prospect of mending these fragile, broken pieces. "Very nice workmanship," he murmurs, holding up a rocking chair that has lost its rocker. "You don't find things made like this today."

"They're old," explains Jane, so seriously that Mama and Daddy both smile.

"Old and beautiful," Mama adds, peering over Daddy's shoulder.

"I wonder if I still have the tools I would need. . . . I think we brought some of the smaller ones with us."

"She said she'd pay you, Daddy," adds Jane eagerly.

"Pay me? I don't know about that, after she's been so nice to you girls."

"Well, we can think about it," Mama says, in the sharp tone that means, "Let's not discuss this in front of the children."

It's not brought up again, at least not in front of the girls. But they notice that in the evenings, after dinner, Daddy spreads newspapers all over the table and starts working on the furniture. He saws, planes, glues, sands, stains, oils, and paints until,

piece by piece, the odds and ends Miss Whitcomb has given them become whole and graceful again.

The days grow dark so early now. Soon it is almost Christmas. Even though there will be no tree, Mama has been saving her pennies and has promised to make a turkey dinner. The children string cranberries and popcorn to decorate the house. Mama says she can use the cranberries to bake and the popcorn for popcorn balls later on—and bits of suet to wind around the trees outside, for the birds. "Even the birds should have Christmas," says Mama.

Jane and Lila think hard about the presents they will give this year. For Mama, they make sachets from their old hankies, dried flowers, and bits of ribbon. A trip downtown to the tobacco shop yields a sturdy wooden box that once held cigars. Lila and Jane decorate it with paint and pictures they have cut out of old magazines. They think it will be a perfect place for Daddy to keep stamps, loose change, and all the other things that fill his pockets. There is still some of the butterscotch toffee left from the box Miss Whitcomb gave them; they will give that to their brothers. "And we'll make pictures for Annabelle," declares Lila. "I'm going to draw her a circus. What about you?" Jane thinks for a moment, crayon poised above the slightly soiled piece of paper she has been saving. "A dollhouse," she says, "because she's never seen one before."

"Silly! How will she know it's a dollhouse and not a regular house?" says Lila.

"Because I'll put all of us in the picture playing with it," says Jane, and even Lila has to admit that this is a very good idea. That leaves only Miss Whitcomb.

"What about a sachet? Like the ones we made for Mama?" asks Jane.

"No, no, it shouldn't be that. It should be something very different and special. Something for the dollhouse," decides Lila. So they ask Mama for her advice.

"Something that you make is always nice. What about a patchwork quilt? You girls could do it together."

"A little patchwork quilt! For Miss Whitcomb's dollhouse!" breathes Jane. "We can't make that," she adds sadly.

"Why not?" says Mama. "I'll help." The sewing basket is brought out; scraps and snippets of fabric are assembled. There are pink-and-white checks and orange and yellow calico, dark green velveteen and pale green linen, tiny ticking stripes, and even a bit of bright red flannel. Mama does the cutting and shows Lila and Jane how to stitch the squares into rows, and the rows together. Mama uses an iron to press back all the tiny seams they have made. "So it won't get all bunched," she explains. Then Lila cuts a backing from a bit of faded blue cloth, and Mama helps her stitch it to the front. The top is left open so that it can be filled with a bit of worn cotton batting, and then the opening is sewn shut. When it is done, neither Lila nor Jane can believe how lovely it is.

They walk over to Miss Whitcomb's the day of Christmas Eve. The quilt, wrapped in a bit of rumpled tissue paper Mama has given them, is tucked safely into Lila's pocket. The branches of the oak trees are covered with snow, and from where they stand it looks as if they are in an enchanted bower of silver and white. "We could play snow princess," suggests Jane, and they do, all the way to Miss Whitcomb's house.

When they get there, they stop outside for a moment. The dollhouse is all lit from within; Miss Whitcomb has placed candles in every window. The tiny wreath with its even tinier holly berries is on the door, and they can see the miniature presents piled high under the Christmas tree in the red-papered parlor.

"Here are my guests!" she greets the girls, who stamp the snow off their boots and move into the warmth. Even though they have grown used to Miss Whitcomb's eccentric clothes, they still marvel at her outfit today: an elaborate black lace dress topped by a black silk shawl. The shawl has long knotted tassels around its edges and is decorated with an embroidered design of purple-and-yellow pansies. Strands of black crystal beads are wound around her neck, and in her hair she wears a glittering tiara.

"Miss Whitcomb!" Jane can't help exclaiming. "You look like a character in a play!"

"Why, perhaps I do," Miss Whitcomb says, smiling. "Now, shall we go and see the dollhouse?" They follow her into the parlor, where Lila hands her the box of furniture that Daddy has mended.

"Look at the work he's put into these things!" says Miss Whitcomb. "They're as good—no, they are better than new! Oh, I must thank him myself. And pay him for his trouble, of course. Did he say how much he wanted?"

"No, he doesn't want to be paid," Lila says. Daddy had made this quite clear when he gave her the box to take over to Miss Whitcomb's. "He said it was to be a gift to you, for taking such good care of us."

"How very kind," says Miss Whitcomb softly. "Except it is you who have taken care of me." Then Lila hands Miss Whitcomb the tissue-wrapped parcel, which she opens very carefully. She is so quiet that for a moment, Lila thinks she does not like the quilt.

"We made it ourselves," she hurries to explain. "Mama helped us. In some places the stitches aren't so straight, but Mama said when it was on the bed, you wouldn't notice."

"We hope you like it," Jane adds shyly. She too worries that perhaps their gift is not fine enough.

"Like it! Why, I love it!" Miss Whitcomb says at last. "Now I have something for each of you. But it won't be ready until tomorrow. Will you come and see me then? And bring your parents and brothers too? My niece from New York is coming in tonight, and we usually have Christmas dinner around one o'clock. Won't you come for dessert? Say, around half-past two? I'm going to serve that brandied fruitcake I remember your father liked so much."

A Cold Christmas

Christmas morning is frosty and clear. The Finney children are up early—Annabelle sees to that no matter what day of the year it is—and they are delighted by the smells coming from the kitchen. Mama is making waffles and bacon. And to their utter shock, there is a Christmas tree in the parlor.

"But how?" exclaims Lila, staring at it in wonder. She recognizes the ornaments as having come from the house on Essex Street.

"You said we couldn't afford one this year," blurts out Henry, equally mystified.

"Well, this one we could afford," Daddy says, beaming. "It was free!"

"Free?" asks William.

"The man who sells the trees gives them away after midnight on Christmas Eve," Daddy explains. "I brought this one back for us." It's a small tree, but shapely, and with the familiar decorations—look, there's the silver glass angel, and over there is the little red Santa—it's positively splendid.

Even more wonderful is the discovery of presents underneath the tree. "Hey, this one is mine!" calls Henry. "Here, this one is for Jane!" and he gets ready to toss it across the room, but Mama restrains his arm. "No throwing in the house," she reminds him, but she is smiling. "Even on Christmas."

The presents turn out to be things Daddy has made from wood; small things, to be sure, but nonetheless the children are thrilled. For William and Henry there are wooden boats. Annabelle receives a wooden duck on a pair of wooden wheels.

There is a string attached to the duck's bill so Annabelle can pull the toy around the house after her. Jane and Lila are given two small wooden doll beds; they immediately decide they will make paper dolls to fit into them.

"Just working on those old pieces inspired me," says Daddy. "I started thinking about what I could do with just little bits of wood." He loves the box Jane and Lila have made—perfect, he says, to keep nails in. And there are other presents too, like the new skirts Mama has made for each of them, using material from a flowered summer dress of hers they have always loved.

With the gifts opened and many thank-yous and hugs exchanged, the Finneys are just sitting down to a big hearty breakfast when they are surprised by a knock at the door. "Who can that be?" Daddy says, tightening the belt on his robe and heading for the front door. When he opens it, no one recognizes the elegantly dressed woman.

"I'm Margaret Whitcomb," she says quietly. "May I come in?" Daddy and Mama exchange worried looks, and Mama says, "Of course" and "How do you do?" Lila and Jane can see clearly that their parents are as puzzled as they are.

"I'm sorry to disturb you, but I have some bad news," she

says, pausing to take a handkerchief from the leather purse she carries. "Aunt Amanda passed away late last night. I know she invited you all over this afternoon and I—" Here she breaks off, crying openly. Jane and Lila both stare at her. They are so shocked by the sight of a grown-up crying that for a moment the news she is bringing doesn't even register.

"Passed away!" Daddy says. "But she wasn't sick, was she? You girls"—he turns to point at Lila and Jane—"just saw her yesterday, didn't you?" They nod dumbly.

"Lila and Jane," says Margaret quietly. "She told me a great deal about you last night. I was so looking forward to meeting you today...." She dries her tears and blows her nose in the handkerchief. "Yes, it was quite sudden. The doctor said it was her heart. She died in her sleep."

Finally the meaning of the words sinks in. Miss Whitcomb is dead. They will not see her today or any other day. Lila cannot quite believe it. Jane is crying now, holding her face in her hands. Mama moves over to soothe her. "I'm so sorry," she says to Margaret. "She meant a lot to the girls, as you can see."

"It was mutual," says Margaret, who hands Mama a box wrapped in green-and-red Christmas paper. "She had this

all ready for them. She would have given it to them today. And this too," she adds, pulling a white envelope from her purse. "She said she didn't know the boys or the baby well enough to choose gifts, so she thought you might use this to get them each something."

Mama slowly opens the envelope and as she looks inside, her cheeks become quite red.

"What a generous lady," Mama says, and now her eyes too fill with tears.

After they have said good-bye to Margaret, the Finneys dress and walk slowly to St. Ann's Church. It is the worst Christmas they have ever had, even worse than the one that came just after Daddy lost his job. It is only when they return home that they remember about the box. Mama gives it to them, and Jane tears off the paper while Lila reads the note that came along with it.

Dear Lila and Jane,

    You said there were no children in the dollhouse, and you were right. Still, I knew there had been some once, and I kept searching in the attic until I found these two dolls, both little girls, from my own childhood. I remembered that I had given them names. The one in the pale pink frock was Juliet and the other, the one who wears amethyst, was Lillibet. Now, isn't that a coincidence— one has the initial J., like Jane, and the other, L., like Lila. So you see they really do belong in some mysterious, magical way to you girls, and I give them to you with love and thanks for many hours so happily spent. Play with them here whenever you like and bring them home to meet your family and your other toys.

                    Your good friend,
                    Amanda Constance Whitcomb

The dolls that Jane unwraps are clearly of the same vintage as the others who live in the dollhouse. They too have delicately modeled bisque faces, real mohair wigs, and the loveliest clothing, all tucked, stitched, and hemmed beautifully. "I can't believe that they're ours," says Jane.

"They'll be able to sleep in the beds Daddy made," says Lila. "They're the right size."

The rest of Christmas day is quiet and sober. Neither Jane nor Lila has much of an appetite for the turkey, the cranberry sauce, the mashed potatoes, and the buttered peas Mama heaps upon the table. They haven't had such a meal in months and months. Still . . .

Before they climb into bed, Lila and Jane make sure to tuck their new dolls into their very own wooden beds. Mama says she will help them sew bedclothes, but for now two of Daddy's handkerchiefs cover the dolls.

"It's so chilly tonight," Lila explains to her sister. "We don't want them to be cold." Jane nods sadly and pulls the covers up around her chin.

The Magic Revealed

The days after Christmas remain bitterly cold, although it doesn't snow again. The girls spend much time indoors, playing with their new dolls. Mama helps them ransack the house for little things they might use in their games: an empty wooden spool is a nightstand, a thimble is a vase for flowers, and a sliding matchbox makes a little trunk. As she promised, Mama helps them make blankets, pillows, and sheets from scraps, though neither of them has the heart to sew another patchwork quilt. Daddy gives them a cardboard shoe box in which to keep everything. When Lila and Jane accompany their parents to Miss Whitcomb's funeral, they bring the dolls with them.

"They'll want to say good-bye to her," explains Lila to Mama and Daddy, who bow their heads in understanding.

Afterward Jane asks if they can walk home along Cheshire Street. She and Lila have not been there since the day before Christmas, when Miss Whitcomb was still alive. When they get to Cheshire Street, they walk slowly; instead of the usual mad dash for the house, Jane holds Daddy's hand and Lila holds hands with Annabelle, who has just recently begun to walk. The house is dark and quiet; for the first and only time the girls remember, the parlor curtains are drawn, hiding the dollhouse.

"That's all right," Lila says to Mama. "I'm not sure I want to see it now anyway. I'd rather think about the last time we were there, with the house all ready for Christmas and everything." They stand in front of the house for a moment before they cut through the oak trees toward home.

It is just a few days after this—New Year's Eve has come and gone—that a crisp white envelope arrives in the mail. It's addressed to Daddy, who is not at home yet, so Mama leaves

it on the table for him. When he gets in, he casually opens it, not caring much about what is inside. All that suddenly changes, and he calls Mama and the girls to hear the letter.

"It's from Miss Whitcomb's lawyer," says Daddy in wonder and surprise. "They're going to be reading her will the day after tomorrow at the house on Cheshire Street, and they want us to be there."

"Us?" says Mama, equally surprised.

"Yes, it specifically mentions that we should be there," Daddy says. "All of us."

"I guess that means she's left us a little something in her will," Mama says slowly. "How very thoughtful she was." She pauses and then adds, "Well, if they want us to be there, we'll be there."

Later, when Lila and Jane are alone, Jane asks, "Do you think it could be the dollhouse? The something that Miss Whitcomb left us?"

"I doubt it," says Lila. "There's her niece, remember? She used to play with it when she was little. I'm sure she'd want it now."

"Oh, you're right. I was just hoping," says Jane, who secretly still is.

✳ ✳ ✳

Unlike the funeral, which was filled with former students and people from the town, the reading of Miss Whitcomb's will is a very private affair, with only the lawyer, Margaret, and the Finneys in attendance. Margaret seems glad to see them all, for she walks up to Mama and hugs her and places a hand on each of the girl's heads. Lila and Jane think she is very glamorous. With her dark red lipstick, tailored gray suit, silk stockings, and high-heeled black pumps, she looks like one of the actresses they see in the picture shows on Saturday afternoons.

"Do sit down," she urges.

Looking around the familiar parlor, the girls see the dollhouse. No one has touched anything since the last time they were here. Mr. and Mrs. Montgomery are seated by the tree; Cassandra, Nanny, Trudy, and the grandparents are standing nearby. The quilt Lila and Jane had made is on the bed upstairs, and the logs Lila had cut are still in the fireplace. Jane wishes that she could go over and play with the house while the lawyer reads various dull things about Miss Whitcomb "being of sound mind and body." But then, the energy in the room suddenly seems different—electric, even. The lawyer is reading these words that even the girls pay attention to:

> *. . . and to my dear young friends, Lila and Jane Finney, I leave my dollhouse and all the furnishings, dolls, and contents within. I know they will love this house as I did and care for it well in the years to come.*

"Mama! Daddy!" Jane cries. "The house! She left us the dollhouse!"

"Yes, she did," Daddy says, looking over at Mama. "But what about Margaret . . ."

"Oh, I don't want the dollhouse," she says. "Where would I keep it? Besides, the house belongs to the children," she continues. "They are the ones who bring it to life."

"What a remarkable lady . . . ," murmurs Mama, but she is barely heard over the noise of the children, for now that William and Henry have seen the dollhouse and understand it is really theirs, they too begin to touch and exclaim over its many enchantments.

"Look, here's a butter churn! The pole moves up and down!" calls out William.

"And the toy trains in the nursery! They actually go round and round!" Even Annabelle joins in; she toddles over to the table where the dollhouse sits and crows, "'Ouse! 'Ouse!" at which the lawyer, Margaret, and all the rest of them start to clap and cheer. Annabelle, who basks in this attention and praise, beams.

When they have all settled down, Mama stands up to embrace Margaret. "What will happen to this house, then?" Mama asks, gesturing around her.

"I plan to sell it. I loved this house as a girl, but my life is somewhere else now."

"It's a lovely house," Daddy says. "Do you think you'll have trouble finding a buyer?"

"I hope not," Margaret says. "I'd like to get back to New York as soon as I can. But first I'll need to empty the house out, I suppose."

"You mean you don't want the furniture?" Mama asks.

"I have a lovely apartment filled with my own furniture now. Of course, there are a few pieces I might bring back with me. But perhaps you might want to take something as well. A sofa or an armchair. Maybe the china service . . ."

"Why, that is so kind of you," Mama says, shaking her head at the offer. "Maybe we will. But first you must show us everything that you want."

"Well, there is one thing that is quite special," says Margaret. "I know just where it is too. I'll be down in a minute." Margaret goes upstairs only to reappear a moment later carrying a covered crystal candy dish in her hands.

"She used to keep this by her bed, filled with treats," explains Margaret. "When I was little, she would always give me some candy from it when I came to visit, and she used it until the day she died. Look, there are still some candies in it." She opens the dish to show Mama. "Butterscotch toffees, her absolute favorites. I used to send them to her from a special shop in New York."

Butterscotch toffees! Mama doesn't understand the significance of this and only says, "It's so pretty." But Lila and Jane look at each other. They don't have to say anything because their look says it all. Then Jane moves over to the dollhouse, and Lila follows her. The boys are chattering away, while Daddy, Mama, and the lawyer talk to Margaret. Annabelle keeps saying, "'Ouse!" softly to herself. "'Ouse! 'Ouse! 'Ouse!"

New House, Old House

"Careful, you're tipping it!" says Daddy to William. "Keep it steady!"

Two days after the reading of the will, the dollhouse is being moved from the house on Cheshire Street to the one on Cottage Road. Lila and Jane have been busy packing up all the tiny treasures in the house. Here is the canopy bed, with the crocheted coverlet; here is the washstand whose top is a piece of real marble. Dishes and books, chairs and rugs, lamps and tables are all wrapped in the tissue paper that Margaret gives them and then placed in cardboard shoe

boxes. The girls use Henry's red wagon to cart everything home. Finally only the empty house remains, and that is what William and Daddy are now carrying carefully along the winter streets. Lila and Jane follow, not helping all that much but not wanting to miss any of the amazing journey either.

People they meet on the way smile broadly when they see the house, and several come to their doors to look out and wave. After all, it's not every day that you move a dollhouse—especially such a splendid old dollhouse—on foot. Even their neighbor's dog, Punch, joins the procession making it seem like a parade.

"I need to rest for a minute," calls William, and after he does, Lila and Jane go over to his end of the house to help him carry it.

Mama is there to welcome them when they arrive home; Annabelle is so excited to see the house again that she runs outside without a coat and starts racing in circles around the little group.

"Come back here, you!" scolds Mama, hurrying after and scooping Annabelle up in her arms. Annabelle gives a cry of protest, but Mama marches her firmly back to the house.

Lila and William are panting from their exertion and run to the sink for a glass of water as soon as the house is safely inside. But Jane just drops to the floor to stare at it. "I can't believe it's really here," she says, touching the roof with her hand. She looks up to see Lila standing over her, a glass of water in her hand. "Hey, don't pour that on me!" she cries, scrambling quickly to her feet. Jane grabs the glass from Lila and drains it noisily.

There is some discussion about where the house is to be kept. At first, Lila and Jane want it in their room. But eventually they agree that the space is too cramped to accommodate it.

"What about in the parlor?" ventures Mama. "After all, we do have the table." Margaret had suggested that they take the long low table Miss Whitcomb had used for the house. The girls look at each other.

"I guess it would be all right," says Lila.

"I know!" says Jane eagerly. "We'll put it in front of the window. Just like Miss Whitcomb did. It will look grand!" Mama and Daddy look at each other, nodding, and Lila smiles. "What are we waiting for?" says Jane. So the table is placed before the windows and the house on its revolving disk is settled on the table. They begin the work of unpacking. But since everyone helps, it hardly seems like work at all.

"I want to arrange the kitchen," says Henry.

"I'll do the upstairs study," William chimes in. Even Annabelle is allowed to join the fun; Lila shows her where to put the canopy bed and the hooked rug that goes on the floor beside it. "Bed!" chirps Annabelle gaily.

After everything is in its place, all the Finneys agree that the house—Miss Whitcomb's house—looks like it fits right in to its new setting. "I just wish she could see it," says Lila a bit sadly.

"Maybe she can," Jane says hopefully. "After all, how can we be sure she can't?"

* * *

As the chill of winter gives way to the melting warmth of spring, the girls have a new reason to hurry home from school. Now the magic of the dollhouse that they always loved awaits them in their own house on Cottage Road. As they hurry up the walk, they can see the house through the shiny windows of the parlor; Lila and Jane take turns polishing those windows so that they are always bright and clear. Once the coats are off, snacks consumed, and homework completed, the house, and all its magic, is theirs.

But one April afternoon, before they turn the corner that leads toward home, Lila stops and puts her arm on Jane's. "Let's go the other way today," she says.

"The other way?" asks Jane. She has a feeling that this is one of those ideas of Lila's that she is not going to like.

"You know," says Lila. "The way we used to go. Along Cheshire Street."

"Oh," says Jane, and there is a long pause. The girls have not walked down that street since the winter day when the dollhouse came to Cottage Road. Instead they have been taking another route home. This was not something that they spoke about. It just seemed to be something that happened.

"I'm not sure I want to," says Jane slowly.

"Me neither," confesses Lila. "But don't you think we should?"

So that is how the girls find themselves walking along Cheshire Street once more. The buds have just started to come out on the trees, though if the girls look up, they can still see the brilliant blue sky through the branches. When

Lila and Jane come to the house they know so well, they stop and stand there quietly for a moment or two, remembering. Then a movement in the front window where the dollhouse used to be attracts their attention. It is a girl. And she is waving at them.

"Do you know her?" Lila asks Jane, for she looks to be about Jane's age. "From your class at school?" Jane shakes her head. The girl continues to wave, so Jane smiles and waves back. Then the girl disappears and a few seconds later reappears at the front door, which she pulls open wide.

"Hello!" she calls out. Now that the door is open, they can see that her shiny black hair is plaited into braids, which have been wound and pinned around her ears. Jane thinks they look a bit like cinnamon buns, but of course she doesn't say this. It's an odd style, but a pretty one, she decides.

"Hello," says Jane, a little hesitantly.

"Is this your house?" Lila asks. The girl nods. When she does, her small dangling silver earrings begin to bob. She has pierced ears. Lila and Jane don't know any girls who have pierced ears, and they are quite envious.

"We just moved in. I don't know anybody here yet."

Then she adds, "How come you stopped? Did you know the girl who used to live here? Was she your friend?"

"We know someone who used to live here," says Lila. "Only she wasn't a girl."

"No? Who was she, then? Maybe you'll tell me about her . . . ?" Lila looks at Jane and shrugs.

"I guess we could," begins Lila.

"Her name was Amanda Whitcomb," interrupts Jane. "She was old. A nice old lady. And she had the most wonderful dollhouse. We came here and played with it all the time."

"A dollhouse?" says the girl eagerly. "I love dollhouses! Where is it? Can we play with it now? I mean, together?"

"It's at our house," says Lila.

"But I thought you said it was here . . . ?" questions the girl.

"It used to be here," explains Lila. "But then Miss Whitcomb died. And she left the house to us."

"Oh," says the girl. "That's too bad." Then after a pause she adds, "So I guess I won't get to see it after all."

"Well, there's no reason why you can't see it," says Jane. "You could come to our house, right now if you want."

"Really?" asks the girl. Lila and Jane both nod. "Let me

just ask my ma!" She runs into the house and reappears a moment later.

"We live on Cottage Road," says Jane as the three girls begin walking together.

"How do you get there?" asks the girl.

"We'll show you," offers Lila.

"What's your name?" asks Jane. "Mine is Jane. And that's Lila."

"Connie," answers the girl. "It's really Constance, but no one calls me that. It's always Connie."

"Constance . . . ," whispers Lila, half to herself. "Wasn't that Miss Whitcomb's name?"

"Was not," insists Jane, who has heard her. "Her name was Amanda. I know because she had the letter *A* monogrammed on her hankies. I remember."

"I meant her middle name. It was in the letter that she sent to us. The one with the dolls." Jane stops walking, and Lila does too. Connie looks from one girl to the other, puzzled.

"Is something wrong?" she asks after a moment.

"No, nothing's wrong," says Lila, linking her arm through Connie's and beginning to walk again. "I always knew it was magic, that's all," she murmurs more to Jane than anyone, who replies softly, "Oh, it is, it is."

Author's Note

The 1920s was a time of record economic growth in the United States. Herbert Hoover was elected president in 1928, and America was thriving. But then on October 29, 1929, the stock market collapsed, an event that ushered in the single worst business depression the United States had ever known. In the months that followed, many wealthy people lost all or most of their money and millions of working people found themselves without jobs and the reasonable hope that they would soon be employed again. For the average family, this meant facing poverty and often homelessness. By 1931 banks in almost every state were either closed or their activities were greatly curtailed; factories were shut, and business itself was paralyzed.

Yet despite these grim statistics, the Depression years were also filled with quiet strength and perseverance as families like the Finneys continued to love and support one another as they struggled to rebuild their lives.

Yona Zeldis McDonough

is the author of *Anne Frank* and *Sisters in Strength: American Women Who Made a Difference,* both illustrated by her mother, Malcah Zeldis. Ms. McDonough has always been intrigued by dollhouses and the magic they possess. She and her two children now enjoy a dollhouse built by her husband. Ms. McDonough lives with her family in Brooklyn, New York.

Diane Palmisciano

has illustrated many books for young readers, including *Hannah and the Whistling Teakettle.* As a child, Ms. Palmisciano was partial to stuffed animals, and it wasn't until she was older that she developed an appreciation for dollhouses. She lives in Cambridge, Massachusetts, with her dog, Daisy.